VEST IN THE
LOAN
don't
let
up
Keep On
Saving Food

This Old THING

WRITTEN WITH GRATITUDE FOR THE MANY SOULS PAST AND PRESENT IN OUR ARMED FORCES. AND FOR JAZ, AURORA, RYDER, AND ALL CHILDREN WHO LOOK UP TO THEM WITH A GLEAM IN THEIR EYE. – C.W.

FOR CHARLES FLOWERS, A GRANDFATHER THAT I NEVER KNEW, AND LIKE SO MANY OTHERS WHO FOUGHT IN THE WAR TO END ALL WARS. AND TO HENRY FULLWOOD, WHO WENT TO WAR WITH A BRUSH INSTEAD OF A GUN. – T.F.

Omnibus Books
An imprint of Scholastic Australia Pty Limited
PO Box 579 Gosford NSW 2250
ABN 11 000 614 577
www.scholastic.com.au

Part of the Scholastic Group
Sydney • Auckland • New York • Toronto • London • Mexico City •
New Delhi • Hong Kong • Buenos Aires • Puerto Rico

First published by Scholastic Australia in 2022.

Design by Nicolette Treanor.

A catalogue record for this book is available from the National Library of Australia

ISBN 978-1-74383-400-8

Typeset in Macaron and Calder.

Printed in China by RR Donnelley.

Scholastic Australia's policy, in association with RR Donnelley, is to use papers that are renewable and made efficiently from wood grown in responsibly managed forests, so as to minimise its environmental footprint.

10 9 8 7 6 5 4 3 2 22 23 24 25 26 / 2

Cassandra Webb *illustrated by* Tony Flowers

This Old THING

AN OMNIBUS BOOK FROM SCHOLASTIC AUSTRALIA

ANZAC day is fast approaching.
If all students could bring
something old
to help our class -

The Herald
Prime Minister
WAR
DECLAR
ENGLAND
War is fast approachin
If all families can giv
young and able to
help our allies
win. On 1 Augu
Germany and
mobilise Bri
Duke

This old thing,

from long ago.

Some memories to keep,

some to let go.

This old thing, from long ago.

What was to follow,

who could know?

This old thing,

from long ago.

So many men, lined up to go.

Weighed up and measured

from top to toe.

This old thing, from long ago.

Worn in the rain

and in the snow.

This old thing, from long ago.

On marched the men,

to and fro.

This old thing,

from long ago.

One last cup

shared with Joe.

This old thing, from long ago.

Duck and crawl, hide down low.

This old thing, from long ago.

Not very interesting. Not much to show.

Just a faded, forgotten, old photo.

This old thing, from long ago.

Us and them

going toe to toe.

This old thing, from long ago.

A silent, deadly, kind of foe.

This old thing, from long ago.

The noise, the tracks,

packed tight, moves slow.

This old thing, from long ago,

Brought with it hope

and sorrow.

This is my great-great-grandad.

He is what I want to show.

AUTHOR AND ILLUSTRATOR NOTE

When my son Ryder was in kindergarten, we visited the Australian War Memorial in Canberra. I, of course, spent most of the time with tears in my eyes as we walked quietly past the poppies and the names. Of the 416,809 Australians who went to war, 60,000 did not return. What particularly gave me a sense of time standing still was the exhibit on Bullecourt where, in 1917, three thousand Australians breathed their last breath. In one of the glass cabinets was a tin mug, the same as what you or I might use when we go camping, with a bullet hole in the side. I wondered if someone was holding that mug when the bullet flew by? I stood for a long time unable to imagine what that would actually feel like. Most of my stories come to me as lines and ideas, and a few of the lines that I left the Australian War Memorial thinking about, eventually became *This Old Thing.*

Cassandra Webb

I found a very personal connection in the story of *This Old Thing.* My grandfather Charles and his brother fought in The Battle of the Somme in 1916. Charles was injured and returned to Australia. He lost his brother Frank on the battlefield. To create the images for this book I wanted to let the reader feel what the world looked like to my grandfather in Europe during World War I. To achieve this, I researched the online archives of the Australian War Memorial and the works of war artist Albert Henry Fullwood. In 1916, the Australian government introduced the 'Australian Official War Art Scheme'. This scheme commissioned Australian artists like Fullwood to join military forces in war times to capture the experience from an Australian perspective. Fullwood's paintings were the inspiration for many of my background images. These paintings were so pivotal in the direction that I took with my illustrations that as a tribute, the main soldier character is loosely based on Fullwood; the character in the story reaches the rank of Sergeant and becomes a medic just as Fullwood himself had done. I added a service dog to my images to help link the child in the present with the main character's story. When we think of times of war, we often forget the large number of animals that have served and supported troops in battle, from pigeons, dogs and horses to the modern-day use of sniffer rats to clear abandoned minefields.

Tony Flowers

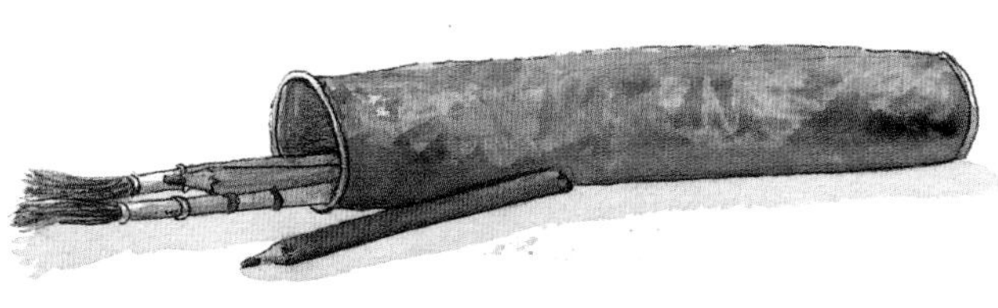

ATTACK
ON
FRONTS